Gramma's Garden

by Barbara Brooks Simons
illustrated by Annabel Kendall

Table of Contents

 C h a p t e r I

The Dream Garden

The late afternoon sun was going down behind the buildings across the street from Josie's house. It turned the sky behind the brownstone townhouses red and gold. The colors reminded Josie of autumn trees, though it was a sweltering, hot summer day. Josie and her brother, Franklin, wiggled on the steps of their front stoop, trying to find a cool spot. They wondered how their grandmother always managed to look cool even on such a hot day. Ignoring the heat, Josie and Franklin turned their attention back to the story that Gramma was telling.

Gramma settled back in her chair. She fanned herself gently and resumed telling her story. "Well, there was a creamy, white fence all around the house and yard. And one big old magnolia tree next to the house. Oh my, that house was a pretty sight to behold."

Gramma continued describing the yard. "First there were sky-blue morning glories. Then we planted hollyhocks. They were a spectacular sight, believe me, in shades of red and rosy-pink and yellow. Why, it was like a rainbow blooming."

Josie and Franklin had heard Gramma's stories many times, but they never got tired of them. There was something so comforting about Gramma's voice. Josie felt like she was being wrapped in a warm, fuzzy blanket when she listened to Gramma's stories. And even though Franklin was 14 going on 15, he still liked to hear Gramma's stories about her life in the South.

Now Franklin got up from the step where he had been sitting. "Gramma, I have to go do my math homework. I'll see you at dinner."

Josie stayed where she was. Like Gramma, Josie loved nature, but living in the city didn't provide much. She looked around the neighborhood. Outside their second-floor apartment, Gramma had planted window boxes, bright with red and white geraniums. Other than that a few spindly trees that grew between the sidewalk and the curb were the only green, growing things that Josie could see.

Other neighbors were sitting on their front stoops, too, hoping for a cool evening breeze. A streetcar rumbled by. Some of Franklin's friends were showing off on their bikes in the street.

"I sure wish you had a picture of that house and garden," Josie said.

"Child, I don't need any picture to remind me," Gramma answered. "I can see it all plain as day in my mind's eye. Flowers for the spirit and herbs for the kitchen. I can even *smell* that garden." She tilted her head back and half-closed her eyes, taking a deep breath.

Gramma's voice was soft, as if she were talking to herself. "There were roses all over. They were the old-fashioned kind of roses, with that rich smell like perfume. We had purple-blue foxglove and delphiniums. Sometimes I'd pick nasturtiums—all yellow and orange—and put them in an old blue china bowl.

"But that garden was for real food, too. We grew scarlet runner beans—pretty red flowers and tasty beans. We had salad greens and tomatoes and beet greens for the pot, too. Nothin' tastes better than fresh greens or tomatoes all warm from the sun!"

Gramma shook her head and let out a loud sigh. Josie knew that Gramma regretted having to leave her garden behind when she and Grandpa moved North more than twenty years ago. Gramma chattered on and told Josie that she and Grandpa had moved North in the 1930s for opportunities. Josie sat up straighter as she knew this part of the story was critical. Gramma and Grandpa had wanted to escape the Jim Crow laws that restricted the black people's lives in the South. Gramma hated that she had not been allowed to drink out of a water fountain or ride at the front of a bus and had to sit in the back of the luncheonette.

Gramma said that things up North were so much better. She and Grandpa could go to the movies. Grandpa got a fine job at a factory, earning good money. And Gramma could sit in the front of the bus as she rode to her daily cleaning job. Then she sighed and Josie knew what was coming next.

"But still I thought there'd be more green around. I love the parks, but I sure do miss my own little plot of land."

Josie jumped to her feet and blurted out excitedly that she had an idea. Josie and her Gramma would plan a garden. Josie raced inside the Williams's apartment. When she came back, she was carrying a drawing pad and a box of colored pencils. For the next couple of hours, until it was dinnertime, she and her grandmother drew busily, making plans and lists.

 Chapter 2

The House

Josie couldn't stop thinking about Gramma's dream. She just had to figure out a way for her family to have a garden. Finally, it dawned on Josie that in order for the family to have a garden, they would need to have a house. Josie liked their neighborhood, but she thought how much better a house with a garden would be.

But how to find that perfect house? One day Josie heard a classmate talking about moving. Her classmate's family had found a house in the newspaper. Josie decided she would check the newspaper.

Every Saturday morning Josie hurried to get the newspaper. She kept her plan a secret. Josie carefully studied all the ads for the perfect house and yard—a yard that could hold a garden.

Then one day she found it. She ran into the kitchen holding the newspaper.

The kitchen smelled of breakfast. Her father carefully pushed his bread past the eggs and sausage and used it to scoop up buttered grits. Her mother and Gramma chatted as they finished their breakfast. Franklin chowed down on eggs and bacon. They all turned to Josie as she burst into the room.

"I've found it! It's perfect!" she said.

Her parents looked up. "Found what? What were you looking for?"

"The house," she said impatiently. "The house with the yard for the garden that Gramma and I want. I found it. You have to call the owners."

Josie's parents looked at each other. A sad look came over her mother's face, and even her Gramma looked upset. Her father immediately began talking and saying that their apartment was just fine. Then Franklin said he couldn't move since his baseball team needed him. Josie's eyes began to fill with tears. Gramma asked Josie to read the ad aloud, and Josie did so in a quavering voice.

"Well, it does sound like a nice house," Mr. Williams said. "I don't suppose it can hurt to look at it." He smiled at Josie. Josie smiled back at her father.

But Josie's mother still looked worried. She spoke quietly to her husband. She asked him if he really thought they could buy a house. A house in a suburb where they might be the only black family. Josie saw her father give her mother's hand a quick squeeze. Gramma looked over. "A phone call won't hurt," she said solemnly. Josie's father agreed and left the kitchen.

He came back and told the family that they had an appointment for this coming Saturday at 1:00. Everyone except Gramma said that they would go. Josie noticed that her mother still had a worried look on her face, though she tried to hide it behind a big smile.

Meeting Mr. Bradley

"Gonna plant a garden, gonna grow flowers." Josie was singing to herself as she picked out one of her favorite dresses. It was blue and white plaid with a full skirt that made her feel special.

When they went out to the car, it was clear that the entire family also felt that this was a special occasion. They weren't "going to church" dressed up, but they were all wearing their good clothes. Josie complimented her parents. Josie's mother gave her a weak smile and adjusted her hat. Franklin, of course, demanded that he also be complimented.

Gramma shooed them on their way. Josie thought she saw a tear dribble down her Gramma's cheek, but decided she must have been wrong. Gramma waved and crossed her fingers behind her back as the family drove away.

After driving about half an hour, they reached the edge of the city. Right away, Josie began counting the trees that lined the streets. She turned to Franklin and loudly proclaimed that she had already counted twelve trees. Her mother told her to settle down. Josie silently kept counting. Her mother seemed nervous and Josie didn't want to upset her. Her father kept asking her mother for directions and he looked nervous, too, but they found the street just fine.

Two large rocks stood on either side of the street like gateposts. The words "Maple Gardens" were chiseled into the stones. "Gardens," Josie whispered to herself. "That's got to be a good sign."

The neighborhood was made up of curving streets lined with trees. The houses were all different colors—green, gray, yellow, white, even a pale blue. Most of them weren't big, but they had neat yards with bushes and flowers and trees.

Mr. Williams stopped the car in front of a house with a For Sale sign in the yard. Josie realized that the house had everything she had been dreaming about.

13

The real estate agent was standing on the front steps of a small gray house, writing in his notebook. He looked up when he heard the car pull up to the curb. But when he saw the Williams family in the car, his eyes got very wide and he dropped his notebook. Before the Williams family could even open their doors, the real estate agent had hightailed it to their car. The speed with which the man moved amazed Josie.

He leaned into the car window, spluttering with anger. His face was very red and his voice shook. "You—you didn't say on the phone that you were black!"

"I guess you must be Mr. Bradley then," Josie's father said in a very soft, but very angry voice. "I shouldn't have to tell you anything about my color. This is America. Skin color's not supposed to matter. I fought in a war for this country. It shouldn't matter whether I'm black or white or polka-dotted!"

The real estate man went on angrily, as if he hadn't even heard a word that Mr. Williams had uttered. He told Mr. Williams that he could get fired for showing them the house. Why, some of the neighbors might come out and throw rocks at them. Mr. Bradley glared at Mr. Williams and asked him in a very low, threatening voice, "Do you want to start a riot? You don't want to see your family hurt, do you?" Just as he finished, Mr. Williams noticed that several men had come out of their homes and were watching them.

Without saying another word, Joe Williams started the car and shoved it into first gear. Josie could see how tightly he clenched his jaw, as if to keep angry words from spilling out. Her mother just looked sad.

Franklin didn't even try to hold back his anger. "We don't need your permission or anyone else's to live where we want!"

Josie looked back at the house. She couldn't hide her disappointment. She started to cry—big, salty tears that felt hot enough to scald her cheeks. "It's not fair, it's just not fair," she wailed.

 Chapter 4

A New Dream

Months went by, but Josie couldn't forget that day, no matter how much Gramma tried to comfort her and tell her that it could have been worse. Josie didn't understand how it could have been worse. That nasty Mr. Bradley had insulted her father and her family. In fact, he'd insulted all black people!

Gramma sighed heavily and told Josie not to carry on so about it. She pulled Josie onto her lap and held her as she whispered that things would get better. Josie wasn't so sure. She didn't have her Gramma's optimism. But as the days wore on, Josie did let go of her anger and disappointment. She truly believed that her Gramma was right when she told Josie that holding onto her anger like that would be giving Mr. Bradley power. And Josie certainly did not want to give that man anything!

One spring afternoon Josie decided to walk home from school. She could save her bus fare to buy a new record. Letting the sun shine on her, Josie decided to take the long way home. As she strolled down a street that she hadn't seen for months, it dawned on Josie that the street had changed.

A rickety old building had once stood on the corner. It had fallen into disrepair. Josie blinked her eyes hard. But no, she was not seeing things, the building had vanished. In its place was an empty lot. Then Josie looked closer—the lot wasn't really empty. Rows of string marked off garden plots with dirt paths that ran between them.

A big sign on the lot read, "Neighborhood community garden. Sign up now!" Several pleasant-looking women were sitting at a card table, taking people's names. A couple of people were waiting in line to sign up. Others were already working on the ground with hoes and rakes. In some plots, little green plants were already pushing out of the ground.

Josie wanted to laugh out loud. Here in her own neighborhood Josie had found her dream. Josie shook her head and remembered that her Gramma had told her to be patient and that things would work out.

Josie stood in line and politely waited her turn. She was so excited she could hardly speak, and when she did the words just raced from her mouth. "Ma'am, I live in the neighborhood and so does my Gramma. My name is Josie Williams, and we both really want a garden, so can just anybody get one?"

The woman at the table looked up and smiled and told Josie that, of course, she and her Gramma could have a garden plot. All Josie had to do was put her autograph and address on the piece of paper in front of her.

Josie scribbled it so quickly that she had to double-check it to make sure she'd written the correct information. This was one time Josie did not want to make a mistake. Then she raced home to get her grandmother.

When the two came back, the smiling woman handed them a little yellow card that read "Plot K14." Gramma and Josie found their plot. Right now Plot K14 was just a bare patch of ground, but as Gramma and Josie began to clear the earth, they pictured hollyhocks and tomatoes—and, of course, roses, all in a blaze of beautiful colors. Gramma suddenly reached over and hugged Josie tightly. Into her ear she whispered, "Hold tight to your dreams and make them come true—whatever you want." Josie promised she would, and the two began to create their dream garden.

Historical Note

While white American families by the thousands moved to suburbs in the 1950s, many real estate developers refused to sell to members of minorities—mainly African Americans and Hispanic Americans. Sometimes neighbors made private "covenants" to keep out minorities. The Civil Rights Act of 1968, often called the Open Housing Act, made such discrimination illegal. Nevertheless, even in the 1970s and 1980s, some families still had to go to court to gain the right to live where they wanted.

Comprehension Check

Summarize

What does Josie want at the beginning of the story? What happens to her dream, and how does she deal with it at the end? Use the Character, Setting, Plot Chart to organize your summary.

Character	Setting	Plot

Think and Compare

1. Look back at page 15. Summarize the reasons Mr. Bradley gives for refusing to show the house to the Williams family. What do his actions show about attitudes and prejudices in the 1950s, when the story takes place? *(Analyze Character, Setting, Plot)*

2. Think about a time when you were treated unfairly, as Josie and her family are in this story. How did you react? What did you do about it? *(Analyze)*

3. From what you have learned about events in American history since the 1950s—for example, the civil rights movement—do you think an incident such as this would be likely to happen today? *(Synthesize)*